The Parallel Room

Haris Alibašić

The Parallel Room

Cover design by: Haris Alibašić

Printed in the United States of America

ISBN-13: 979-8-9954339-2-7 (Hardcover)

ISBN-13: 979-8-9954339-0-3 (Softcover)

ISBN-13: 9798995433910 (eBook)

For those who carry futures with no destination.

TABLE OF CONTENTS

INTRODUCTION

The Loss of the Future

Heartbreak rarely announces itself as an ending. More often, it arrives as a quiet recalibration of time.

The day continues as scheduled. The body functions. Thought proceeds. Yet something essential no longer points forward in the same way. What disappears is not only a person, nor even the intimacy shared with them, but the *future that had already begun to exist internally*. A future rehearsed in thought, adjusted in feeling, and accepted as plausible—sometimes even inevitable.

This book begins from that loss.

It arrives quickly, intensely, illuminated by attention and affirmation. It constructs a future at high speed—through words, gestures, promises, and emotional proximity—only to withdraw without explanation. Silence replaces presence. Absence replaces language. The future collapses not because it was disproven, but because it was never formally revoked.

What remains is a particular kind of grief: not for what was, but for what had already begun to feel *on its way*.

This book is about that grief.

It examines heartbreak as the loss of access—not only to a person, but to a shared trajectory. The pain does not stem solely from abandonment or rejection. It stems from the sudden erasure of a world that had already been mentally furnished. Conversations imagined. Ordinary rituals anticipated. A life quietly assembled in advance of its arrival.

When that future disappears without explanation, the mind does not know where to place it. Memory holds it, but memory has no temporal authority over what never formally occurred. The result is a form of heartbreak that resists completion.

This resistance is not pathology. It is coherence seeking resolution.

The heart continues to feel.
The brain continues to search for narrative.

The soul continues to recognize meaning where social reality has withdrawn permission.

Heartbreak, in this sense, is not a rupture between heart, mind, and soul. It is their continued collaboration in the absence of confirmation – a command to attention where none exists.

The book unfolds in the space created by that association.

It does not argue that love bombing is misunderstood kindness, nor that silence and ghosting are ambiguous. It treats sudden emotional withdrawal for what it is: a destabilizing event that removes both presence and explanation. Yet it does not focus on blame. Blame provides too much closure. The deeper wound lies elsewhere.

The deeper wound is the disappearance of the *future self*—the version of oneself that had already begun to exist in relation to another.

That self does not vanish simply because the relationship ends. It remains internally active, unfinished, and unacknowledged. It appears in moments of recognition, in light, in places, in habits that no longer have a destination.

This is where the parallel world begins. The hidden rooms open.

The interior world that emerges after such heartbreak is not fantasy in the escapist sense. It is an adaptive structure. It allows the mind to continue what reality interrupted: integration, coherence, meaning. In this world, conversations reach clarity. Silence acquires explanation. The future is reassembled—not as expectation, but as memory of what *might have been.*

The beauty of this world does not lie in denial. It lies in restraint.

The beloved is not forced to return. The relationship is not rewritten as ideal. The imagined coexistence respects the finality of separation while refusing the erasure of significance. Love continues, but without entitlement. Presence persists, but only as light—reflected, refracted, and diffused across perception.

This book treats that interior labor with seriousness.

It refuses the cultural demand that healing must look like forgetting. It rejects the idea that emotional maturity requires amnesia. Instead, it explores the dignity of those who continue to carry love thoughtfully, even when it no longer has a place to land.

Heartbreak, here, is not weakness.
It is the consequence of having constructed a future sincerely.

What follows is not a confession, nor a therapeutic guide. It is a study of how people remain human after intimacy dissolves—how they continue to see, to feel, and to imagine, even when the world no longer mirrors their inner coherence.

This book is written for those who lost not only someone, but a future that had already begun to feel remembered.

CHAPTER ONE

The Future That Arrived Too Early

She did not enter my life quietly.
She entered it as presence.

Not dramatic presence, not spectacle, but something more disarming: *availability*. She was there without hesitation. Responses came quickly. Questions assumed continuation. Affection arrived without the protective delays that usually precede trust. It felt less like seduction and more like alignment.

I remember thinking—without saying it—that this was what ease felt like.

The messages started immediately. Not scattered across days, but woven through hours. Morning greetings before I had formed thoughts. Questions about my day while it was still unfolding. She remembered details—small things I mentioned in passing, preferences I didn't realize I had shared.

It felt like being seen with high-resolution attention.

How did you sleep?
Did that meeting go well?
I was thinking about what you said yesterday...

Each message carried the implicit assumption that we were already connected, that continuity was obvious. There was no testing period, no cautious escalation. Intimacy arrived fully formed, as though it had been waiting for permission to exist.

I found myself responding in kind. My replies grew longer. I began sharing things I normally kept private—frustrations with my book publisher, forebodings about politics in the country, thoughts that felt too unfinished to speak aloud. She received all of it without judgment, without advice, just... presence.

I understand that.
That's true, I agree.
Tell me more.

The future assembled itself without ceremony. It did not arrive as plans, but as orientation. I found myself speaking as though time ahead had already been agreed upon.

Ordinary sentences carried assumptions inside them. *When we do that. Next time. You'll see.*

Nothing felt premature because nothing felt forced.

We met for coffee on a Tuesday afternoon. She arrived early, already seated when I walked in, and the smile she gave me contained no performance. Just recognition, as if we'd been doing this for years. She asked about my work, my research, my music. She listened the way people rarely do—leaning forward slightly, eyes focused, asking follow-up questions that proved she'd been paying attention.

She was someone who smiled across a faculty meeting once and whose presence had lingered in memory like a bright bookmark. She waves me to the table.

"You write a lot huh? And produce under HAR!S, right?" she said. "I looked you up. That darkstep track you released last month—it's heavy. I love it."

No one had done that before. No one I dated had cared enough to find my writings and music, to listen, to have an opinion.

At night, alone, I replayed conversations not to revise them but to inhabit them again. The way her voice softened when she spoke about things she cared about. The way affirmation arrived fully formed, without strategic caution. There was no negotiation for closeness. It was granted.

This is how trust forms when it forms too fast: it feels like recognition rather than risk.

One night, she called me late. Past midnight. Her voice was quieter than usual.

"I can't sleep," she said. "Can we just talk?"

We talked for three hours. About nothing urgent. About everything. Childhood memories, embarrassing moments, dreams we'd abandoned and ones we hadn't. She told me about a relationship that had ended badly, how she'd learned to protect herself, how tired she was of being careful.

"I don't want to be careful with you," she said. "Does that make sense?"

"Yes," I said. Because it did.

I noticed the internal shift before any external marker. My mind began placing her in future moments without my permission. I imagined her reactions to things that had not yet happened. I caught myself preparing explanations for decisions I had not yet made, as though she were already entitled to them.

When I traveled for a conference, I bought her something small from the airport—a bookmark with a quote from Rumi. She loved poetry. She'd mentioned it once. I remembered.

When I gave it to her, her eyes got bright.

"You were thinking about me?"

"Constantly," I admitted.

She kissed me then. Not tentatively. With certainty.

That was the moment the future crossed from possibility into memory.

Then one evening, she texted: *I'm not feeling well. Think I'm getting sick.*

I showed up at her apartment with soup, tea, medicine, ginger, green bananas. She opened the door looking exhausted, and something in her face softened when she saw me.

"You didn't have to do this," she said.

"I wanted to," I replied.

I stayed. Made sure she ate. Sat with her while she rested. She fell asleep on the couch, her head against my shoulder, and I didn't move for two hours because moving would have meant disturbing her.

When she woke, she looked at me with something I can only describe as wonder.

"No one has ever taken care of me like this," she whispered.

A few days later, she took me to dinner. Insisted on paying.

"You took care of me," she said. "Let me take care of you."

The restaurant was small, intimate, candlelit. We shared food bites. She told me about her family, her fears, the things she wanted from life. She asked about my faith, my prayers, my relationship with silence.

"I want to appreciate and understand you," she said.

The next week, she gave me a compass.

Small. Silver. Precise.

"So you can pray at my place," she explained. "I know it matters to you. I want you to be comfortable here."

I held that compass like it was a covenant.

On a Saturday, we went to a record store. She wandered through the vinyl, pulling things out, reading liner notes.

She stopped at a Nine Inch Nails album—*The Downward Spiral*—and held it for a moment.

"I love this one," she said quietly, then put it back.

The next day, I went back alone and bought it.

When I gave it to her, she stared at it, then at me.

"You remembered."

"Of course I remembered."

She pulled me close and whispered against my neck: "I don't know what I did to deserve you."

We made love that night—urgent, tender, consuming. Afterward, we lay tangled in sheets, her fingers tracing patterns on my chest.

"This feels real," she said.

"It is real," I replied.

The future did not need to be imagined. It appeared spontaneously.

We talked about travel. About music festivals we could attend together. About introducing each other to our parents, children—carefully, when the time was right. About small rituals we might build. Morning coffee. Evening walks. Shared silence.

Nothing felt rushed, yet everything felt inevitable.

One night at the movies, during a moment when the screen went dark between previews, I turned to her.

"Will you be my girlfriend?"

She smiled. Kissed me.

"Yes."

We sat through the film holding hands, passing popcorn back and forth, whispering jokes to each other. Laughing quietly. Connected.

When I dropped her off, she kissed me again, longer this time.

"Text me when you get home," she said.

I did.

She responded immediately: *Goodnight. I'm so happy.*

Then the texture changed.

It did not announce itself. There was no rupture. Just a faint delay. A message read but not answered. A familiar rhythm interrupted by silence that did not explain itself. At first, I accommodated it. People get busy. Lives expand. Attention fluctuates.

I told myself all the reasonable things.

But reason does not dismantle momentum. It lags behind it.

The next day, I sent a message: *Hope you're having a good day.*

Hours passed. No response.

Then: *Busy. Talk later.*

But later never came.

The silence lengthened. Not erratically, but cleanly.

It had form. Discipline. It felt chosen.

I remember opening my phone repeatedly without expectation, only habit. The body reaches before the mind accepts. Each time, the same quiet screen. No anger. No confusion yet. Just absence behaving with intent.

Inside, conversations began.

Did I misunderstand something?
Did you mean everything you said?
At what point did it change for you?

I did not imagine her answers at first. I waited for them. I rehearsed calm explanations I would offer if she returned. I practiced restraint. I did not want to appear reactive.

I sent one more message: *Is everything okay? You seem distant.*

She replied hours later: *Fine. Just need some space.*

Space. The word carried no timeline, no boundary, no explanation.

I gave her space.

Days became a week. A week became two. The silence was absolute. Disciplined. As if she had decided with precision that I no longer required acknowledgment.

Time passed. The future remained intact.

That was the unbearable part—not longing, but persistence. The future refused to collapse. It stayed vivid, active, unresolved. I could feel it inside me, still organizing my expectations, still preparing me for something that no longer had a point of entry.

At some point, I stopped waiting and began speaking to her in my head.

You could have said anything, I told the imagined version of her.
You could have said this is too much, too fast, too soon.
You could have said you changed your mind.

In my imagined conversations, she listened. She did not interrupt. She allowed me to finish.

In those moments, I was not trying to bring her back. I was trying to complete something that had been left structurally unfinished. Silence had suspended the sentence of us mid-thought.

I replayed moments with forensic attention. Not searching for guilt, but for coherence. The way she said my name. The way she leaned into certainty. The way she spoke as though continuity were obvious.

Did you know you were leaving when you said those things?
Or did you mean them only in the moment they were said?

The imagined version of her did not defend herself. She simply existed as presence again. That alone was enough to steady me.

This is where the parallel world formed—not in fantasy, but in necessity.

In that world, conversations ended properly. Silence had reason. I did not revise reality. I acknowledged it fully. She was gone. But the future was allowed to finish becoming what it had already started to be, only now without her consent or participation.

I lived both worlds simultaneously.

In the external world, I functioned. I spoke to people. I worked. I smiled at the appropriate moments. Nothing in my life signaled collapse.

Internally, I carried an intact future with no destination.

The images arrived uninvited. Light through a window at a certain hour. A phrase overheard that matched her cadence. A laugh that landed too close to memory. She appeared not as herself, but as interruption—as recognition without object.

The compass sat on my desk. The Nine Inch Nails vinyl remained on my shelf. The bookmark from Rumi stayed in the book where I'd placed it. Physical evidence that something had been real.

The imagined conversations changed over time. At first, they were explanatory. Later, they became quieter.

Eventually, I stopped asking why.

Not because I understood, but because the question had exhausted its usefulness. What remained was not confusion, but loss of access. I could no longer be with her. I could no longer become who I had already begun to be alongside her.

That was the heartbreak.

Not the absence of her body.
Not even the absence of her voice.

But the disappearance of the future that had already taken up residence inside me.

And every day since, I have lived with that future—neither denying it nor expecting its return—allowing it to exist as light rather than destination.

That is how I learned to remain intact without resolution.

CHAPTER TWO

The Room Where Time Waits

The room always appears the same way.

I enter it without crossing a threshold. One moment I am elsewhere—lying awake, sitting at a desk, standing in a kitchen—and then I am there. The transition leaves no mark. The room does not announce itself. It simply receives me.

Light comes from the left, angled low, as though afternoon has decided to remain suspended. It does not move quickly. Shadows lengthen almost imperceptibly. The walls are pale, unadorned, free of memory. This matters. Nothing here belonged to us before.

The air has a quality I cannot name. Not cold, not warm. Neutral. Patient. As if temperature itself has learned restraint. When I breathe, the sound doesn't echo, but it doesn't disappear either. It exists, then fades at a pace that feels intentional.

The table sits in the center—not symbolic, simply present.

Wood grain visible but unremarkable. Two chairs, facing each other across a space that feels measured. Not close enough for intimacy. Not far enough for estrangement. The distance is calibrated for truth.

She is already seated when I arrive.

Not expectant. Not surprised. She sits with her hands folded loosely in front of her, as though she has been waiting without counting the time. There is a chair across from her. It has always been there.

"You came," she says.

Her voice is calm. Familiar. Untroubled by what has passed between us.

"Yes," I say. "I didn't mean to. It just happened."

I move toward the empty chair. My footsteps make no sound, but I feel the floor solid beneath me. This is not a dream. Dreams float. This has weightiness.

She nods, as though this explanation is sufficient.

Time in the room does not demand efficiency. Silence expands without discomfort. Outside this place, silence always felt like refusal. Here, it feels like permission.

I sit. The chair is solid beneath me. My hands rest on the table. I notice the grain of the wood, how it swirls in patterns that suggest age without decay.

"I don't understand when it changed," I say finally. "I keep going back over it."

She looks at me without defense. Her eyes are clear. Not sad, not apologetic. Just present.

"You're looking for the moment you lost access," she says.

"Yes."

She considers this, then shakes her head slightly.

"There wasn't a moment," she says. "There was a decision not to explain."

The light shifts. Not dramatically—just enough to signal time passing without consequence.

The shadows on the wall lengthen by degrees. Minutes or hours, I cannot tell. The room does not recognize that distinction.

"Why not say anything?" I ask. My voice does not rise. Anger does not survive well here. "You knew what you were building."

She pauses. Her fingers move slightly on the table, a small gesture I recognize from memory—the way she used to think before speaking.

"I knew what I was feeling," she replies. "I didn't know how long it would last."

"That didn't stop you from speaking in futures."

"No," she agrees. "It didn't."

The honesty steadies me more than an apology would have.

I look around the room. There is a window now, though I do not remember it appearing. Beyond it, light thickens and thins, like breath. No landscape. No buildings or trees. Just duration made visible.

The quality of light suggests late afternoon stretching into evening, but the transition never completes.

"I built something," I say. "Quietly. I didn't rush you. I didn't ask for guarantees. I just... adjusted."

I think of the compass. The vinyl. The late-night phone calls. The way I rearranged my schedule to be available when she needed me.

"I know," she says.

"How do you know?"

"Because I felt it happening," she replies. "And I let it."

Silence returns. It sits between us, but it does not erase either of us.

I realize then that this is what I had needed: a silence that remains shared. Not the punitive silence of her absence, but something that acknowledges presence without demanding speech.

Outside the room, days move aggressively forward. Here, time pools. It gathers without evaporating. I could stay here indefinitely, and the world would continue without me. That knowledge should be frightening. Instead, it's stabilizing.

"I don't want you back," I say. The sentence surprises me with its truth. "I just wanted it to end properly."

She leans back slightly, the chair responding to her weight. The movement is small but audible in the stillness.

"Properly would have required me to stay longer than I could," she says. "Or leave sooner than I did."

"So you chose disappearing."

"I chose not to undo what had already happened," she says. "Even if that meant leaving it unfinished."

I close my eyes briefly. Behind my eyelids, I see the restaurant where she took me to dinner. The record store. Her apartment, our time together at my house, or my office, where the compass still sits somewhere, forgotten or discarded. When I open them, she is still there. This continuity matters more than resolution.

The light dims a fraction. The room adjusts. The walls seem to breathe—expanding slightly on the inhale, contracting on the exhale. Or perhaps it's my own breathing reflected back to me.

"What happens now?" I ask.

She smiles—not warmly, not coldly. Just accurately.

"Now you keep the future," she says. "Without me."

I feel the truth of it immediately. The future does not vanish. It transfers. It becomes interior. All those plans we half-made, all those conversations we anticipated—they still exist. Just reconfigured. Relocated to a space where her participation is no longer required.

I stand. She does not.

"Will you still be here?" I ask.

She pauses. The light catches her face at an angle that makes her seem both present and distant simultaneously.

"I'll appear when you need coherence," she says. "Not comfort."

I nod. That distinction holds.

When I leave the room, there is no door. The light remains behind me, steady, unoffended by my absence. The walls do not protest. The table and chairs remain arranged, waiting for the next time coherence becomes necessary.

Later—hours or days afterward—I find myself in the world again. Streets, voices, obligations. But something has changed. The future no longer presses forward blindly. It exists somewhere I can visit, where time waits, where silence does not erase meaning.

That room remains.

And I understand now that it was never about keeping her.

It was about keeping myself intact in the absence of explanation.

CHAPTER THREE

Time Bends, Memory Speaks

The room is the same, yet it is never the same.

I enter and find her sitting at the table as always. Afternoon light diffuses softly through the invisible window. Shadows stretch long and deliberate. But something is different: I see the same table from three angles at once—the way it looked yesterday, the way it will look tomorrow, and the way it stood when she first appeared in the room.

The air shimmers slightly, as if reality itself is uncertain which version to present.

I speak, but my voice arrives in layers.

"You came," I say—but I hear it three times. Once with relief. Once with resignation. Once with something closer to accusation.

She smiles. "Yes."

But the word echoes, multiplying across temporal registers. I hear her say it the way she used to—bright, immediate, full of certainty. I hear it as she might say it now—cautious, distant. I hear it as it might sound in some unreachable future—tender, impossible.

I sit. The chair responds differently in each moment. The one from yesterday creaks softly, bearing the weight of repetition. The one from tomorrow is silent, as if anticipating my presence. The one from the first meeting fits perfectly, molded already to my shape, as though it had been waiting years for me to arrive.

"I don't understand when it changed," I say, in all three temporal registers simultaneously.

The words overlap but remain distinct. Past frustration. Present confusion. Future acceptance. All true. All inadequate.

She listens. She always listens. That's what makes this room bearable—she cannot leave mid-sentence here. Cannot go silent while I'm still speaking.

"Do you ever stop asking?" she says, her voice layered over itself. The echo is not confusing. It is illuminating. I hear patience in one layer, fatigue in another, and something like tenderness in the third.

"No," I admit. "I think about it constantly. Every moment, every word."

I remember texting her good morning every day for three months. I remember her responses—always quick, always warm. *Good morning, you. Hope you slept well. Thinking about you.* Then one morning, nothing. The next morning, still nothing. The silence arrived without warning, without diminishment. Full presence to full absence in a single unacknowledged transition.

"Every moment is already layered," she says. "You think the past is gone, but it is still speaking. You think the future is denied, but it is only waiting."

I look at her, at three versions of her, at a hundred reflections across time, and try to respond. The light in the room fractures into bands—gold, amber, pale gray—each representing a different temporal layer. They don't blend. They coexist.

"I built a future quietly... and now it's fractured. I can't live there or here fully."

I think of the night I bought the Nine Inch Nails vinyl. How carefully I wrapped it. How her face looked when she opened it—genuine surprise, genuine joy. *You remembered.* Of course I remembered. That's what you do when someone matters. You pay attention. You remember the small things because the small things are everything.

"You are already living there," she says. "You just need to recognize it. The room, the conversations, the light—these are not substitutions. They are continuations. The fracture is part of the architecture."

I close my eyes. I see the moment she first appeared, vivid and immediate. The coffee shop. Her smile. The way she leaned forward when I spoke, as if my words were the only thing that mattered in the world.

Then I see yesterday—three months after her silence began. The room darker, shadows stretched differently, my chair creaking beneath my weight, the conversation heavier, saturated with exhaustion.

Then I see tomorrow—the light slightly cooler, and I am older, quieter, steadier. Still here. Still carrying this. But different somehow. The burden distributed more evenly.

I open my eyes. The three timelines are still visible, still overlapping. The table exists in all of them simultaneously. The walls breathe at different rates—quick and shallow in the past, slow and deep in the present, barely perceptible in the future.

"And if I leave?"

"You will carry it," she says. Her voice overlaps itself again, layered: a warning, an invitation, a recognition. "The fracture moves with you. You do not lose it. You inhabit it differently, but it remains intact."

I stand, noticing the floor beneath me simultaneously smooth, worn, and unmarked. In one timeline, countless footsteps have polished the wood. In another, I am the first person to walk here. In another, the floor has no history yet, waiting for my presence to mark it.

The walls are unchanged, yet their angles shift subtly with my awareness. The window reflects three skies at once: bright afternoon, muted dusk, and the deep gray before dawn. I understand, suddenly, that the room is not about her. It is about me and the versions of myself that live within absence.

"You were always part of it," I say. "Even when you were gone."

"Yes," she says. "And even in the silence, you were not alone. You were speaking to yourself, to the versions of yourself that needed completion. I am only the echo you needed."

I think of the compass. How it sits in my desk drawer now, unused but not discarded. Sometimes I take it out, hold it, remember the way she handed it to me. *So you can pray at my place.* The small weight of it. The care embedded in that gesture. How do you throw away evidence that someone once cared?

I sit again, in all three temporal layers, and for the first time, I do not feel the absence as emptiness. I feel it as continuity.

The three versions of the room merge slightly. Not completely—they remain distinct—but they touch at the edges. The light from one timeline bleeds into another. The sound of my breathing in the past harmonizes with my breathing in the present and future.

I speak quietly. "Then I will stay here. Not to bring you back. Not to relive. But to be with what was already built."

She nods, layered and singular, and the room breathes with me. Light shifts slowly, deliberately. Shadows stretch. Time bends but does not break. The fracture is no longer pain; it is lens, prism, vessel.

And in that space, I begin to understand that the future, though fractured, has never been lost. It simply waits for acknowledgment—and the courage to inhabit it without apology.

The conversation ends. Not definitively. Not permanently. But it exists across all its temporal echoes. The room holds it, and in holding it, I learn that absence does not erase. It illuminates.

The three timelines begin to separate again as I prepare to leave. The past version of the room grows slightly dimmer. The future version brightens fractionally. The present remains exactly where it is—neutral, patient, waiting.

I leave. The floor beneath me is the same, yet different. The light lingers. The fracture remains—and for the first time, I see it as gift rather than wound.

CHAPTER FOUR

The Myth of Replacement

The city does not know what I have lost.

It performs itself with confidence—people moving with intent, conversations overlapping, lights changing on schedule. Cafés fill and empty. Strangers lean toward one another with temporary intimacy. Everything suggests continuity. Everything insists that what ends is meant to be replaced.

I walk through it carrying the quiet expectation that this is what I am supposed to do next.

Replace.

The word appears everywhere once I start noticing it. Not spoken directly, but implied. In advice. In tone. In the way people tell stories about moving on as though intimacy were modular—one unit removed, another installed.

Find someone new.
Meet someone else.
You'll see, it will feel different.

As though difference were the same as repair.

The sidewalk is crowded. Bodies flow around me like water around stone. A couple passes, hands linked, leaning into each other as they walk. The gesture is casual, unremarkable to them. To me it's a reminder of what the body remembers—how her hand fit in mine, the specific pressure of her fingers, the way she'd squeeze twice quickly when she was happy about something.

I sit in a café I have never been to before. Deliberately chosen for its unfamiliarity. The light is wrong—too sharp, too declarative. Fluorescent and unforgiving where I need something softer. The table is small, circular, chrome-edged. Modern. Sterile. There is no chair across from me that feels intentional. Still, I choose a seat that faces the door, a habit I did not know I had developed.

The barista calls out orders in a voice that cuts through conversation. Someone laughs too loudly. Music plays at a volume designed to fill space without demanding attention. Everything here is engineered for turnover, for efficiency, for the next customer.

I imagine her there.

Not vividly. Not sentimentally. Just accurately enough to notice the mismatch. She does not belong here. This light would have irritated her. She preferred dimmer spaces, candlelit corners, places where shadows could gather. The room we shared—the other room, the one that exists outside geography—would not tolerate this light.

A woman at the next table laughs. The sound lands with precision—bright, musical, unguarded. For a moment, my body responds before my mind does. Recognition without object. My head turns automatically, expecting to see her.

It's not her. Of course it's not her. Different hair, different face, different everything. But the laugh carried the same frequency, the same unself-conscious joy.

I look up, expecting nothing, and feel the echo anyway.

This is how the parallel world asserts itself.

Not by pulling me backward, but by interrupting the present with alignment. My body still searches for her in crowds, in sounds, in the quality of light at certain hours. Three months later and I'm still calibrated to her presence.

I hear the word *replacement* again, this time from a stranger behind me. I cannot see him. I only hear the word, detached from context, floating briefly before dissolving into noise.

"...just a replacement for what she really wanted..."

The timing is too exact to ignore. Not meaningful in the cosmic sense, but meaningful in the way coincidence becomes legible when the mind is already fractured. Synchronicity is not prophecy. It is attention sharpened by loss.

I imagine saying it to her.

"They think I want a replacement," I tell the version of her that walks beside me now, just out of step with my body. She's there—not visibly, but as a presence I carry. A voice that responds in my internal dialogue.

She does not look surprised. In my imagination, she never is. She knows me too well. Or knew me. Past tense still feels wrong.

"You're not looking for a person," she says. "You're looking for access."

"Yes," I reply silently. "Access to the future that closed."

"That future was specific," she says. "It won't reopen just because someone else arrives."

We pass a bookstore. Inside, people browse with the quiet seriousness of those who believe meaning can be found if they stay long enough. I stand outside and watch my reflection in the glass, layered with shelves and spines and movement behind me.

My reflection is tired. I notice this with clinical detachment. The kind of tired that sleep doesn't fix. My face looks the same as it did three months ago, but something has shifted in the arrangement. My eyes hold differently. My mouth sits in a neutral position that suggests permanent caution.

I think about how often replacement is confused with continuation.

A replacement assumes equivalence.
What I lost was singular.

Not because she was irreplaceable as a person, but because the future we built together was non-transferable. It was designed for us alone. Its measurements do not fit another body.

I remember the night she gave me the compass. We were at her apartment. She'd just finished making dinner—pasta with a sauce she'd learned from her grandmother. We ate on her couch, plates balanced on our knees, some documentary playing that neither of us was really watching.

Afterward, she disappeared into her bedroom and came back with a small box.

"I got you something," she said.

The compass. Silver, precise, beautiful in its simplicity.

"So you can pray here," she explained. "I know it matters to you. I want you to be comfortable in my space."

The future that gesture implied—me praying in her apartment regularly, my presence there normal, expected, welcomed. A future where my spiritual practice was not an inconvenience but something she wanted to accommodate.

That future had specific dimensions. It required her apartment, her willingness, her sustained interest in my comfort. You cannot transfer that to someone new. You cannot say to another woman, "I need you to care about where I pray in your apartment" and expect it to carry the same weight.

I sit on a bench and watch the afternoon shift toward evening. Light behaves differently now—closer to the light in the room where time waits. For a moment, the boundary thins between the two worlds. I could slip into that interior space right now, mid-afternoon on a city bench, and no one would notice.

"I could meet someone tomorrow," I say to her, knowing she's not really there to hear it but saying it anyway. "It would not touch this."

"No," she agrees in my imagination. "It would start something else."

"And that would be fine," I say. "Just not as replacement."

She stops walking—or my mental version of her stops. I stop too, in the real world, standing in the middle of the sidewalk while people flow around me.

"People replace roles," she says. "They don't replace futures."

The sentence settles into me with the quiet authority of something already known. This is what I've been trying to articulate for three months. The ache is not for her specifically—though I miss her—it's for the architecture we built. The routines we established. The unspoken agreements. The way she'd text me when she was having a hard day, knowing I'd respond. The way I'd send her music I was working on, knowing she'd listen. The way we'd make plans three weeks out with the confidence that we'd still want to see each other when the date arrived.

You cannot recreate that infrastructure. You can build something new, but it won't have the same foundation, won't bear the same weight, won't mean the same thing.

This is the real loss: not her absence, but the impossibility of substitution. The future I imagined does not migrate. It remains where it was last coherent, intact but closed. Like a house you once lived in that someone else occupies now. The address still exists. The rooms are still there. But you can never go back.

I do not resent this.

Understanding it relieves me of urgency. I no longer scan rooms looking for her outline in other bodies. I no longer mistake chemistry for continuity. I begin to let encounters be what they are instead of auditions for repair.

As I walk home, the city feels less hostile. Still indifferent, but no longer instructive. I do not need it to teach me how to replace what was never designed to be replaced.

The evening air is cooler. Street lights begin to flicker on, one by one, illuminating the path ahead in measured intervals. I think of the compass again, sitting in my drawer. I think of the vinyl record on my shelf. I think of all the small objects that carry the weight of gestures, of care, of a future that was real for exactly as long as it was.

That night, I return briefly to the room.

She is not there.

The chair across from mine remains empty, and for the first time, it does not accuse. The emptiness is just emptiness—neutral, patient, without judgment. I sit anyway. The light holds. Time behaves. The walls breathe their slow, steady rhythm.

I understand now that replacement was never the task.

The task was integration.

To carry what was built without forcing it to be lived again.

To allow new futures to arrive without asking them to heal old ones.

To recognize synchronicity not as guidance, but as confirmation that meaning still responds to attention.

The room does not disappear.

Neither does the city.

They coexist now—parallel, communicative, no longer in conflict.

And I walk between them without needing to choose.

CHAPTER FIVE

Dinner, Diffusion, and the Impossibility of Replacement

The restaurant smells of roasted garlic and olive oil. Glasses clink at neighboring tables. The air carries warmth, conversation, and something faintly aspirational—people attempting to be present in the moment. I enter carrying the light from the room where time waits, like a secret ballast.

She is waiting. Not the woman I lost, but someone new and yest someone known to me for a long time. Someone who smiled across a soccer field once where our kids played together and whose presence had lingered in memory like a bright bookmark. She waves me to the table.

"Glad you came," she says. Her voice is calm, courteous, inviting. Nothing frantic. Nothing rehearsed.

I sit. The chair feels ordinary. I notice how ordinary it feels. Ordinary is both relief and risk.

"I hope you like this place," she says. "I chose it because it's quiet but not too quiet."

"I appreciate that," I say.

But my mind, of course, is already elsewhere. The room where time waits flickers in the periphery of vision. The parallel future pulses there, untouched, untouchable. I think of the last time I sat across from someone at dinner with intent—the night she took me out to thank me for caring for her when she was sick.

That dinner was at a small Italian place she'd been wanting to try. She'd made the reservation weeks in advance, back when weeks in advance still felt like a reasonable timeframe for us. We'd share small bites of food.. She'd told me about her childhood, about her mother who taught her to cook, about the grandmother whose recipe she'd used when making me dinner. About kids and her ex-husband.

"You took care of me," she'd said that night. "No one ever does that."

And I'd believed her. I'd believed that my care mattered, that it was building something, that attention given was attention that would be returned.

"Are you okay?" the woman across from me asks now, pulling me back to the present restaurant, the present moment.

"Yes," I say. "Sorry. Long day."

We order. Sparkling water – she remembers - I don't drink alcohol – never did. Light dishes. Small talk begins. She tells me about a conference she's attending next month, about a project she's working on. I listen, genuinely interested, but there's a part of my consciousness that's monitoring itself, tracking my responses, making sure I'm present enough but not too present, engaged but not presumptuous.

"I have a boyfriend," she mentions casually, as though it were air itself. "He travels a lot for work, so I make dinner dates with friends when he's gone. Just... company."

I notice how easily she says it. How matter-of-fact. How her presence does not retreat or apologize. She is herself. Singular. Independent. Unavailable.

I nod. "Of course. That makes sense."

It does not unsettle me. Not really. But the parallel world insists on whispering reminders: replacement is impossible. Continuity cannot migrate. The future built in absence remains unbreeched.

The waiter brings food. She smiles at him—the same smile she gave me when I arrived. I realize it's just how she moves through the world. Warmly. Openly. Not specific to me. This is both comforting and clarifying.

"So," she says, cutting into her pasta, "how has your week been?"

"Busy," I say. "Teaching, working on some research. Playing a few sets this weekend."

"Oh, that's right—you DJ. What kind of music?"

"Electronic. Darkstep, drum & bass, some tech house. Depends on the venue."

"That must be such a release," she says. "Getting to be creative in a completely different way than your academic work."

"It is," I agree. And it's true. The DJ stage is one of the few places where the fractured timelines don't intrude. When I'm mixing, I'm fully present—reading the crowd, feeling the bass in my chest, anticipating the next transition. For those hours, there's only now.

"You know," she says, twirling pasta around her fork, "I think you would take care of me. If I needed it. You seem like someone who shows up."

The comment catches me off guard. Not flirtatious—observational. Like she's noticed something about how I move through the world.

"I try to," I say carefully.

"We don't see each other often enough," she continues. "Outside of soccer matches and training sessions for kids. It's nice to actually talk."

She means it kindly. Acquaintance to acquaintance. Friend to friend. But the words echo differently in my head because someone else once said something similar, in a different context, with different gravity.

No one has ever taken care of me like that.

That was her. My ex. The night I showed up with food and medicine when she was sick. The way she'd looked at me when she said it—vulnerable, grateful, certain that this meant something permanent.

"You seem thoughtful," the woman across from me observes now, pulling me back. "Not sad, exactly, but... elsewhere."

I smile faintly. "I suppose I carry multiple times at once."

She laughs softly. "That sounds exhausting."

"It is," I admit. "And necessary."

She nods, sipping her sparkling water. The acknowledgment does not pity. It recognizes.

We continue talking. She tells me about her projects, about a trip she's planning, about a hiking journey she took last summer. I contribute where appropriate, ask questions, maintain the rhythm of conversation. And yet, every exchange is punctuated by an unspoken fact: she is not mine, and she never could be. She is whole and external. Her boundaries are precise, her life in motion, and in motion she remains singularly inaccessible.

I catch myself imagining variations—alternate meals, alternate evenings. What if she were single? What if the timing were different? What if I were different? But even in imagination, I know they are not replacements. Each scenario fractures under its own weight.

The compass sits in my desk drawer. The book I received from my ex sits on my shelf. The dinner she bought me is a memory I revisit but cannot recreate.

This dinner, pleasant as it is, builds nothing. It confirms nothing. It simply exists as itself—two friends sharing a meal, filling time, exchanging pleasantries.

"I like being able to share a meal without expectation," she says suddenly, as if reading the echo of my attention. "No pressure, no agenda. Just... company."

Exactly. That is what is happening here. Company, not continuation. Observation, not substitution. The lesson crystallizes in dialogue: the women I meet are themselves. They are full lives, autonomous, unavailable for the futures I once imagined. The room where time waits remains intact, untouchable by new bodies.

Dessert arrives. Chocolate mousse for her, espresso for me. She takes a spoon, tastes it, closes her eyes briefly in appreciation. The gesture is innocent, complete, entirely her own. I am witnessing it, not participating in it.

The room flickers again in my mind—light, shadow, conversation layered over itself, multiple temporal echoes. I carry it all. The synchronicity of dessert, of light, of motions, the repetition of dialogue—everything merges into a pattern I do not control. And yet, there is peace in observation. In seeing without needing to possess. In recognizing beauty without demanding access to it.

Dinner ends. Payment is made—she insists on paying for it. We leave the restaurant together but separately, walking toward our cars parked in different directions.

"Thank you for this," she says. "It was really nice."

"It was," I agree. And I mean it.

We part with a brief hug, the kind friends give. Her perfume lingers for a moment—lavender, maybe, or something floral I can't name. Nothing like what she wore. Nothing that triggers memory. Just scent, pleasant and temporary.

I drive home in silence, no music, just the hum of the engine and the occasional rush of passing cars. The parallel world is quiet tonight. Not absent—never absent—but content to wait.

No replacement has been found. None is needed. Only integration of awareness, of presence, of observation.

I return home. The room waits. Time waits. Light waits.

And for the first time, I realize: the parallel world is not an escape. It is preparation. It is training the mind to inhabit absence without being diminished. It is witnessing without possession.

And that, I think, is the only replacement that ever truly matters: the capacity to live fully in the fracture.

CHAPTER SIX

Mirrors in Motion

I am at the jiujutsu class, waiting in the hallway. The mats smell faintly of disinfectant and sweat, sunlight bouncing off polished floors. Parents lean against the walls, phones in hand, bags at their feet. Children move in circles, practicing controlled falls and rolls. The noise is steady, predictable, rhythmical.

My son is on the mat, his small body learning how to redirect force, how to fall without injury. I watch him with half my attention, the other half already drifting to that interior space where thoughts spiral and memories replicate themselves endlessly.

Then I see her.

Not her. Not exactly.

A woman standing near the edge of the mat, adjusting her child's belt, glasses sliding slightly down her nose.

The same posture. The tilt of her head when she bends to speak. A way of leaning in just enough to be attentive, without collapsing herself into the moment.

For a fraction of a second, the air halts.

She is a replica. A ghost, a possibility, a light that refuses to extinguish. I catch myself thinking—instinctively, unbidden—*her*. The mind wants closure, wants a conversation. But nothing occurs. There is no introduction, no recognition. We are not connected. The resemblance is enough. It is too much.

The glasses are what do it. Wire-rimmed, delicate. She used to push hers up the same way when she was thinking, when she was reading something on her phone and trying to maintain the conversation simultaneously. It was a small gesture I loved—evidence that she was fully engaged in multiple streams of attention, never quite able to turn off her mind.

I remember one night, late, lying in her bed after we'd made love. She was wearing those glasses, and nothing else, reading something on her laptop, her hair falling forward. I'd asked what she was reading.

"Article about neural plasticity of AI and Machine learning," she'd said. "Trying to understand how we adapt to loss."

The irony of that now is almost unbearable.

I take a breath. Step backward slightly. I do not approach. I do not speak.

Her child practices a throw. She watches, quietly, hands folded, glasses catching light at the edge of the mat. I notice the curve of her cheek. The way her hair catches under the gym lights. The cadence of attention in her movement—the same cadence I once knew intimately.

My thoughts swirl. Almost dialogue.

You're not her.
And yet you are.
Why does this echo feel like a hand on my shoulder that isn't there?

Time elongates. Seconds stretch into minutes. The jiu-jitsu moves continue.

Boys and girls fall, rise, spin. Instructors call out corrections in patient voices.

Parents nod, clap, whisper encouragement. But the replica of her holds a different gravity. She is both present and unreachable.

I imagine what a conversation would be like.

Hi.
Hello.
You look familiar.
You remind me of someone I lost.

And then I stop. None of it occurs. None of it is needed. The tension, the echo, the recognition—the glance—is enough. It lingers. It folds itself into memory.

The woman adjusts her glasses again. I notice the small gesture—the same one my ex used to make when thinking, when speaking, when simply existing beside me.

It is amplified here because no words intervene, because no movement completes the pattern.

She catches me looking. Our eyes meet for less than a second. There's no recognition there—how could there be?

We're strangers. But in that brief exchange, I see something I recognize: a kind of watchful tiredness. The look of someone who has also learned to carry burden invisibly.

Or maybe I'm projecting. Maybe I see what I need to see because the alternative is that I'm simply staring at a stranger in a jujutsu hallway, making her uncomfortable with my unintended intensity.

I shift my weight. My son calls to me from the mat—"Dad, did you see that?"

I respond, but my eyes drift back, tracing her shape among the light and shadow.

A small smile flickers across her face as her child completes a throw. It is ordinary. It is banal. It is perfect.

She has no idea she looks like someone who devastated me. She's just a mother watching her kid learn martial arts, probably thinking about what to make for dinner, or whether she remembered to pay a bill, or any of the thousand mundane concerns that fill a day.

Nothing happens. Nothing can happen.

The class ends. Parents collect their kids. Bags are shouldered. Shoes are retrieved. The woman helps her child with their jacket, straightens their collar, and walks toward the exit without looking back.

I leave the hall a few minutes later, my son chattering about a technique he learned.

The image of her, or her replica, remains suspended in my mind. I replay it, not as memory, not as hope, not as fantasy—but as an observation. A presence that exists because attention noticed it.

The echo endures.

That night, lying in bed, I see her again—not the woman from jiujutsu, but the original. The one whose glasses I used to steal playfully, putting them on to see how the world looked through her prescription. Everything slightly blurred, slightly off, but bearable for a moment.

"Give those back," she'd laugh, reaching for them.

"Make me," I'd say.

And she would. She'd climb on top of me, pin my wrists, retrieve her glasses with exaggerated triumph. Then she'd kiss me, and the playfulness would shift into something else, something heavier and more urgent.

Days later, I will see the same gesture in sunlight, in the tilt of another woman's head, in a reflection passing in a store window.

Each recurrence will not replace her, will not complete a sentence left unfinished. But each will be a reminder: **the parallel world is not imaginary. It is enacted in attention, recognition, and the quiet acknowledgment of presence without possession.**

The hallway empties. The mats lie still. The light shifts. And in that stretch of absence, I feel the room waiting, the fracture steady, and the possibility of coherence—not resolution, not repair, but integrity in suspension.

CHAPTER SEVEN

The Sideline

The soccer field opens wide, too wide for what I am carrying.

Children run in uneven lines, chasing a ball with seriousness disproportionate to the moment. Parents line the sideline, folding chairs, coffee cups, sunglasses perched with practiced indifference. The sun presses down, flattening shadows, erasing subtlety.

I stand near the fence, slightly apart from the other dads and moms. This is my son's team, but I am not integrated into the parent social structure. I arrive, I watch, I leave. Polite nods exchanged but nothing more.

That is when I notice her.

She is married—I know this without knowing how. The ring is there, yes, but it is not the ring that tells me. It is the posture.

The way she stands slightly apart from the other parents, mirroring my own isolation. The way her arms cross and uncross, as if unsure where they belong. Beauty is present, unmistakable, but muted, disciplined, held in check by something heavier.

She has blonde hair pulled back in a ponytail, aviator sunglasses hiding her eyes. Athletic build. Yoga pants and a faded university t-shirt. She could be any suburban mother at any soccer game in America. Except.

Except for the sadness.

It radiates from her like heat. Invisible but perceptible. The way she watches the game but doesn't really see it. The way her phone stays in her pocket even though everyone else is constantly checking theirs. The way she shifts her weight from foot to foot, as if standing still requires too much effort.

She glances at me.

Not long. Not inviting. Just long enough to register presence.

I feel the recognition before I understand it. Not attraction exactly. Curiosity mixed with sorrow. Her face carries something unresolved, something lived with rather than spoken. She watches the game, but not closely. Her eyes drift. They return to me briefly, then away again.

We do not smile.

That would be too much.

The moment stretches because nothing fills it. No conversation. No context. Just awareness. I imagine the parallel room flicker into existence—not because she belongs there, but because the sensation is familiar. The recognition of another person carrying heaviness quietly.

I wonder what she has lost.

Or is losing.

Or expects to lose.

I wonder if she wonders the same about me.

The game continues. A child falls, gets up. A parent shouts encouragement that sounds more like instruction. The referee's whistle cuts through humid air.

She watches, or pretends to. Her jaw is tight. Her shoulders carry tension that has nothing to do with whether her child's team wins or loses.

A goal is scored. Parents clap. She does too, but her clapping is delayed, slightly out of sync, as though she is applauding something else entirely. A different victory. A different survival.

I imagine saying nothing to her.

And that is exactly what happens.

I think about the last time I stood on a sideline with her—not this woman, but the one I lost. It was a different sport, a different field, but the same quality of suburban weekend ritual. We'd brought coffee, stood close enough that our shoulders touched, and she'd leaned into me when the air got cool.

"This is nice," she'd said. "Just being here. Together."

"Yeah," I'd agreed. "It is."

And it was. The simplicity of it. The ordinariness. Standing on a field watching boys play, drinking mediocre coffee, making quiet jokes about the overly competitive parents. Building a life out of moments that didn't demand grandeur.

That future—the one where we stood on sidelines together, where "we" was an assumption rather than a question—that future dissolved without ceremony. And now I stand alone, noticing other people's sadness because my own has made me fluent in recognizing it.

The woman glances at me again. This time I meet her eyes—or I think I do, through the sunglasses. There's an exchange there. Wordless. Mutual acknowledgment that this space does not permit more. The sideline is not designed for truth. It is designed for supervision.

The game ends. The whistle blows. Players collapse dramatically on the grass, as if they've just completed a marathon. Parents gather their things.

She gathers hers quickly. Efficiently. No lingering. No small talk with other parents. She collects her child, straightens their jersey, and walks toward the parking lot without looking back.

The sadness remains intact. So does the beauty. Nothing is exchanged, and yet something has passed between us—a mutual acknowledgment that this space does not permit more. The sideline is not designed for truth. It is designed for supervision.

I watch her walk away, carrying whatever she arrived with. The set of her shoulders. The careful way she places one foot in front of the other. The child beside her, oblivious, chattering about the game.

The loss here is not hers or mine.

It is the loss of possibility itself.

And that, I realize, is a quieter grief than heartbreak, but no less persistent.

My son runs up, sweaty and grinning. "Did you see my assist?"

"I saw it," I say. "Great pass."

We walk to the car. The field empties behind us. The sun continues its descent. Somewhere, that woman is driving home to a life I will never know, carrying sadness I recognized but could not name.

The parallel room does not open for her. She remains in the world of facts—married, present, surviving. But for a moment, we occupied the same quality of silence. And that silence, brief as it was, confirmed something I already knew.

We are all carrying futures that closed without our permission.

CHAPTER EIGHT

The Sterile Proximity

The gym smells of rubber mats and disinfectant. Music pulses overhead, relentless, anonymous. Bodies move with intention but without intimacy. Everyone is focused inward, or pretending to be.

I choose a bench and sit. The weight rack in front of me is organized with precision—dumbbells arranged in ascending order, each in its designated slot. Everything here is designed for isolation, for individual effort, for the pursuit of improvement without collaboration.

She arrives moments later.

I cannot place her. Brazilian, Japanese—my mind searches for geography, for origin, for narrative. But none of that matters. What matters is the way she occupies space. Calm. Balanced. Unselfconscious.

She is stunning.

Not in the dramatic sense. In the precise sense. As though beauty has settled into her rather than announced itself. Her hair is pulled back in a sleek ponytail. Her posture is upright. She wears simple athletic clothes—black leggings, a gray tank top—but they fit her like they were designed specifically for her body.

She sits beside me, close enough to register warmth, far enough to maintain formality.

The bench is long enough for three people, but we're the only two here. She sets down a water bottle, pulls out her phone, scrolls briefly, then sets it aside. She stretches quietly, methodically, as if following an internal rhythm. One arm across her body, then the other. Neck rolls. Shoulder rotations. Each movement deliberate, controlled, beautiful in its efficiency.

I feel the impulse to speak.

It rises quickly and is immediately disciplined.

This is not a place for beginnings.

Gyms are transactional spaces. Efficient. Sterile. People come here to work on themselves, not to intersect meaningfully with others. Any attempt to breach that order feels invasive, almost unethical.

Still, the impulse lingers.

I imagine a sentence forming. Something neutral. Something harmless.

"That's a great stretch for shoulder mobility."

"Have you been training here long?"

"Mind if I work in between your sets?"

But I also imagine how it would land—awkward, misaligned, intrusive. A violation of the unspoken code that governs this place. Silence is the contract here.

She glances at me briefly.

Not curious. Not dismissive. Just aware.

Our eyes meet for a fraction of a second. Enough to confirm that we are both present, both noticing, both restrained. Her eyes are dark, intelligent, unreadable. Then she looks away, returns to her stretches.

The parallel room appears again—not because she belongs there, but because my mind has learned to respond to proximity with construction. It builds worlds quickly now. It invents futures as reflex.

In that imagined space, I speak to her. We have a conversation. She tells me her name, her story. I tell her mine. We discover commonalities, shared interests. We exchange numbers. We meet for coffee. A future assembles itself with the speed and clarity of something inevitable.

I stop it.

Not forcefully. Gently.

She finishes stretching, stands, walks away without looking back. Her absence is immediate, clean.

No residue. No lingering sadness. Just the quiet confirmation that this was never meant to be anything more than proximity.

I watch her move to the squat rack across the room. She loads the bar with practiced efficiency—two plates on each side, clips secured. She steps under the bar, lifts it onto her shoulders, descends into a perfect squat. Her form is flawless. She performs her sets with focused intensity, resting precisely ninety seconds between each one.

She is complete unto herself. Self-contained. Her workout has a logic and rhythm that requires no external input. She is not here looking for connection. She is here doing work that is hers alone.

I return to my own workout. Shoulder press. Rows. Deadlifts. The familiar burn of muscle under load. The music continues its relentless pulse. The mirrors reflect nothing new except the truth I already know: some encounters exist solely to test restraint.

Between sets, I see her again in the mirror. She's moved to a different machine now, adjusting the weight with quick, confident movements. She catches me watching, or maybe she doesn't. It's impossible to tell with mirrors, with angles, with the way attention works in spaces like this.

The bench cools where she sat. I touch it briefly—not with any romantic notion, just noticing temperature, the evidence that someone was here and now is not.

And I understand now that these sterile spaces—sidelines, gyms, waiting rooms—are not failures of connection. They are **boundaries**. They protect what is unfinished from being prematurely misdirected.

There is dignity in leaving things unspoken.

There is integrity in walking away intact.

I finish my workout, return my weights to their designated places, wipe down the equipment.

She's still there when I leave, focused on her final exercises, earbuds in, completely absorbed in her own process.

Outside, the afternoon air is humid. The parking lot shimmers with heat. I sit in my car for a moment before starting it, letting the temperature equalize, feeling the residual adrenaline of the workout settle in my muscles.

The parallel room is quiet. No one inhabits it right now. It waits, patient as always, for the next moment when coherence becomes necessary.

But for now, this moment—sterile, bounded, preserved—is enough.

CHAPTER NINE

The Room of Potentialities

The room waits.

I enter. Light falls differently now—lower, softer, as if acknowledging that time has already passed, that observation has matured. Shadows linger longer along the walls, gathering quietly in corners where absence collects. The chair across from mine is empty, yet present, as though expecting me.

I sit.

The wood grain of the table is more visible now, or perhaps I'm simply paying closer attention. Each swirl and knot tells a story of growth, of years accumulated in silence. The table has weight, substance. It demands presence.

I hear her voice before I see her.

Not a voice of words exactly, but a tone I recognize. It carries rhythm, implication, echo.

"You came back," it says. Not accusation. Not greeting. Just recognition.

"Yes," I say. "I needed to see."

She appears, slowly, without urgency. She sits across from me. The chair resists the weight of expectation, creaks slightly under the impossibility of her being here and not being here simultaneously. The room stretches. Silence becomes the medium through which we communicate.

"I am not here to explain," she says.

"I know," I reply. "I am not asking."

But that's not entirely true. Part of me still wants explanation. Part of me still believes that if I could just understand the mechanism of her withdrawal, I could metabolize it, could file it away in a place where it wouldn't keep burning.

We watch the light together. It moves as if to remind us that time is never absent, even here.

The walls seem slightly thinner than before, allowing glimpses of possible futures: corridors I could have walked with her, empty streets where we might have lingered, doors I might have closed differently.

I see us at a music festival. She's dancing, eyes closed, completely absorbed in the sound. I'm watching her, memorizing the way her body moves, the way joy looks on her face. Later, we're in a tent, rain drumming overhead, talking about nothing and everything. Building intimacy through shared duration.

I see us cooking together in her kitchen. She's telling me about her grandmother's recipe, measuring ingredients by feel rather than precision. I'm chopping vegetables, badly, and she's laughing at my technique but not correcting it. Just letting me be imperfect in her space.

I see us introducing each other to our friends—carefully, slowly, with appropriate structure. A casual lunch or dinner, coffee, a game night.

Building something larger than just us, a future that includes the people we're responsible for.

All of these futures shimmer in the periphery of the room, visible but untouchable.

"I keep thinking about what could have been," I say. "Not the past exactly... the future I imagined with you. It's a kind of loss I cannot name."

She tilts her head, acknowledging. The gesture is familiar—the way she used to think before speaking, weighing her words.

"Future loss is heavier than past loss," she says. "The past is done. The future was always optional."

I consider this. "Optional... but contingent on us. On reciprocity. That delicate balance of attention, intention, presence. And now, it's gone. Taken away without ceremony. Without explanation. That is the part that lingers."

She nods. "It does not vanish. It exists in the space you hold for it. Potentiality does not die; it simply remains unrealized."

I breathe slowly. The room bends slightly with the cadence of my thought.

I imagine the conversations we might have had, the plans, the gestures that never happened. I imagine reciprocity—the symmetry of intention between us—fractured, now irretrievable.

"What lies beyond?" I whisper. "Beyond this room, beyond presence, beyond the fracturing?"

"Nothing determined," she says. "Nothing fixed. Only observation. Only what you carry forward. The weight of reciprocity remains, but it is yours to witness, not to demand."

I close my eyes. I see the room populated by futures that never were: dinners we never attended, streets we never walked, hands we never held after that first month. I hear the echoes of laughter, fragments of conversation, moments suspended like dust in light. They do not resolve. They do not conclude. They simply are.

I remember the three-hour phone call. The one where she told me she didn't want to be careful with me. The way her voice had sounded—vulnerable, hopeful, certain.

The way I'd felt afterward, lying in bed unable to sleep because my whole nervous system was vibrating with possibility.

I remember buying the Rumi bookmark. Standing in the airport gift shop, reading through different quotes, choosing the one that felt most like what I wanted to say to her. *"In your light I learn how to love. In your beauty, how to make poems."* Simple. True. Perfect.

I remember her texting me at 2 AM once: *Can't sleep. Thinking about you.*

And me responding: *Good thoughts or bad thoughts?*

Her: *Very good thoughts. Come over?*

The invitation. The trust embedded in it.

The assumption that I would drop everything, drive across town at 2 AM, because that's what people do when they're building something real.

And I had. Of course I had.

I open my eyes. She is still there, calm, without judgment.

The chair across from mine continues to wait. I realize that this is not grief, exactly. It is **contemplation of absence with full acknowledgment of its integrity**.

"Do you exist here?" I ask. "Or am I inventing you to make sense of what is gone?"

She smiles faintly. "I exist in your attention. And your attention exists in the future you imagine. That is sufficient."

I nod. The room stretches further. Time pools around us, neither moving forward nor collapsing backward. The light shifts subtly, catching edges of the space I had not noticed before—small details, grain in the walls, the way shadows collect differently in each corner.

I lean back. "It feels... wrong to hold onto this."

"It feels wrong only because the world outside demands linearity, completion. Here, the world is as it always was: layered, contingent, partial. Nothing is missing. Nothing is lost. Only... unclaimed."

I consider this. And for the first time, I realize that the parallel room does not exist to resolve absence. It exists to **reflect it**, to probe it, to allow me to inhabit the tension between presence and non-presence without needing restitution.

"The compass," I say suddenly. "Do you remember giving it to me?"

"I remember," she says.

"What were you thinking when you did that?"

She pauses. In the real world, she never answered questions like this. She deflected, changed subjects, moved laterally. But here, in this space, she can afford honesty.

"I was thinking that I wanted you in my life," she says. "Permanently. That compass was me making a commitment I didn't know I couldn't keep."

"Why didn't you know?"

"Because I believed my feelings were facts," she says. "I believed that intensity was the same as sustainability."

The answer doesn't heal anything. But it provides structure.

A framework for understanding that doesn't require agreement or forgiveness.

We sit together. Silence thickens, stretches, resonates. The room does not demand a conclusion. It allows potentiality, impossibility, and reciprocity to coexist.

And in that coexistence, I feel something I had not before: not peace, not closure, not release—but a deep calibration. A recognition that **the future I imagined, the reciprocity I lost, the moments unclaimed—they continue to shape the observer**.

The chair remains. She remains. And I, for a while, simply exist alongside both.

CHAPTER TEN

The Dream of the Room

The room waits, but it is no longer the room.

Walls ripple, fold inward, then stretch wide. Light fractures into dozens of narrow beams, each catching dust motes that float like suspended stars. Shadows no longer obey geometry; they curve, loop, intersect. Chairs multiply, half empty, half occupied. I see myself in each one, breathing differently, thinking differently, remembering differently.

She is everywhere and nowhere. One version sits across from me. Another leans against a window I do not remember. Another walks along the perimeter, tracing shapes with her fingers in the air. I hear echoes of her voice, layered upon itself, murmuring sentences I both know and invent:

"You cannot hold the future, only inhabit it."
"You are here and not here, seeing and unseeing."
"The fracture is your companion now."

I attempt to speak. Words splinter into fragments before they reach her ears.

I miss you. I remember. I am here.

Each iteration of myself repeats the sentences differently, in different tones, in different times. Some are accusatory. Some tender. Some absurdly neutral. All coexist.

The room has become infinite. Doors appear and disappear. Some lead to memories—I see her apartment, the restaurant where we first kissed, the record store where I bought the vinyl. Others lead to futures that never happened—a shared home, a vacation we planned but never took, a lazy Sunday morning that exists only in imagination.

I move between chairs. One moment I sit beside the version of her I loved, the next I stand beside a version I never met, a version who is laughing at something unspoken. The room bends. The ceiling tilts. The floor curves upward.

Time stretches and snaps like elastic, moments repeating with small variations—her smile just slightly slower, her hair catching the light at a different angle, her eyes reflecting versions of me I do not recognize.

I imagine the conversations we might have had. They multiply infinitely. The "what ifs" echo:

- What if I had stayed silent instead of speaking?
- What if she had explained, even minimally?
- What if I had walked away immediately, or never walked at all?
- What if there were no absence, only continuation?

The questions form geometric patterns in the light. They hover, rotate, intersect. I attempt to answer them. Answers fracture again, becoming multiple versions of me giving contradictory responses. One says *You would have failed anyway.* Another says *You would have thrived.* Another says *It does not matter, it simply exists.*

I see new presences in the room. They are neither her nor me. They are echoes, specters, impossible versions. The woman from the jujutsu class is here, adjusting her glasses.

The sad woman from the soccer field stands in a corner, arms crossed. The beautiful woman from the gym performs perfect squats in slow motion.

Each holds a potentiality, a fragment of memory, a shadow of conversation. I cannot name them, but I recognize their weight. Some lean toward me; some recede. Some repeat words I never spoke. Some are still.

A version of the chair across from me tilts forward. I sit, or I think I do. The floor under me disappears. Light passes through me. I do not fall. The room holds me, suspends me. Fractured walls reflect fractured selves.

A version of her—one I never imagined—leans across the table and smiles faintly.

"You are learning to carry absence," she says, in multiple voices at once. "You do not repair. You do not reclaim. You do not replace. You inhabit."

I nod, though I feel as if I have nodded a thousand times already, each nod slightly different.

The echoes of my own voice whisper across the room, repeating, correcting, contradicting.

I'm learning.
I'm failing.

I'm surviving.
I'm drowning.
I'm becoming something new.

All true simultaneously.

I step toward the edge of the room. Or perhaps I float. The walls dissolve further. Time stretches into infinity. I see myself in a thousand rooms, each with her in a thousand forms. Each room reflects every conversation, every glance, every silent acknowledgment. Each fracture becomes a lens through which I perceive what is lost, what persists, what was and what might have been.

In one room, we're still together. Happy. The compass sits on her nightstand, used regularly. The vinyl spins on her record player. We've met each other's parents and friends. We're planning a trip to Morocco. The future we imagined has become the present we inhabit.

In another room, we never met. I am alone but unburdened. The weight I carry doesn't exist because the relationship never happened. I am lighter, simpler, less fractured. But also less. Diminished by the absence of what I learned through loving her.

In another room, she explained. Gave me the courtesy of language, of reason, of closure. The ending still hurts, but it makes sense. I can file it away, metabolize it, move forward without this constant rehearsal of unanswered questions.

In another room, I'm the one who leaves. I sense her pulling away and I exit before she can shut me out. I protect myself, preserve my dignity, refuse to be the one left behind. But I carry guilt instead of confusion, wondering if I abandoned something salvageable.

The rooms multiply. The versions proliferate. My mind cannot hold them all, but it tries, stretching itself thinner and thinner across infinite possibilities.

And then, for the first time, I sense **a calm calibration**: the fractures are not chaos. They are structure.

The splintered light, the multiplied selves, the recursive conversations—all are architecture. I no longer ask why. I do not seek resolution. I do not demand continuity.

I merely **inhabit** the space.

The room, multiplied infinitely, breathes with me. Time bends. Memory pulses. Absence glows with presence. And for a moment, exquisite, unexplainable, the fractures themselves feel like home.

All the versions of her speak at once: "This is where you live now. Not in one timeline, but in all of them. Not in certainty, but in possibility. Not in what happened, but in what it means."

I understand. Or I think I do. Or I will, eventually, when the dream releases me.

The light intensifies. The rooms begin to collapse back into one, slowly, like a reverse explosion. The chairs return to their singular forms. The walls solidify. The floor becomes solid again beneath me.

But I know now: the fracture is permanent. The multiplication is real. I will always carry these versions, these possibilities, these unrealized futures.

And that is not a curse.

It is architecture.

CHAPTER ELEVEN

Sleep and the Dreamed Room

I lie down.

The ceiling above bends subtly, as if breathing with me. Shadows twist in slow spirals. The room stretches, contracts, folds into itself. Sleep arrives not as darkness but as **a continuation, a deeper layer of reality**, where memory, absence, and imagination dissolve into a single continuum.

I am present, yet untethered. The chair across from me is gone. Light no longer behaves predictably. Instead, it flows like water, pooling in corners, spilling across walls, refracting into shapes I recognize and cannot name.

She is here, or perhaps all the versions of her. She leans closer, leans away, smiles, sighs, disappears. Every version of the room we have inhabited flickers through my vision: the parallel room, the gyms, the sidelines, the cafés. They overlay, intersect, and blur. Boundaries collapse.

A voice, familiar yet impossible, whispers: "You carry absence like gravity."

I feel it in my chest, in my throat, along the spine of every imagined self. The absence weighs, yet sustains. I move through the dream as if walking a hall of mirrors. Each reflection is a memory, a possibility, a fragment of time. Some mirrors show laughter we never shared. Some show streets we never walked. Some show dinners never eaten, conversations never held, glances never returned.

One mirror shows the night she gave me the compass. But in this version, I refuse it. "I can't accept this," dream-me says. "It implies a future you can't guarantee." She looks hurt, confused. The future fractures differently. We end sooner, with less pain but also less meaning.

Another mirror shows us five years in. Married. Integrated. The love-bombing phase long past, replaced by something steadier, more sustainable. Or maybe duller. Maybe the intensity that drew us together was always destined to consume itself.

Another mirror shows her at my funeral. I've died somehow—heart attack, car accident, the specifics don't matter. She's there, crying, telling someone "I never should have left him." But it's too late for should-haves. Too late for anything except regret.

I try to speak. Words fracture midair. *I remember. I miss. I see.* They echo, layer, contradict, multiply. I feel them collide with versions of me I have never met.

A corridor opens. Light pours through it, liquid and cold. Shadows gather at the edges. I walk. She follows. Or perhaps I follow her. Perhaps we walk side by side without touching, without speaking, without recognition necessary.

The corridor becomes a beach. Night time. Waves crash with rhythmic insistence. She walks ahead of me, footprints appearing in wet sand, immediately erased by water. I try to catch up but the distance remains constant. I call her name but the wind takes my voice.

I glimpse figures in the periphery. Married women, strangers, women who could have been replacements, versions of the Brazilian-Japanese woman in the gym—all present, all absent. Their faces reflect pieces of what was, what could have been, what may yet appear. None intersect fully with me, yet all ripple across the surface of consciousness, like stones dropped into a vast, still lake.

The dream expands. Reality bends beneath it. A hallway becomes a field. A field becomes a room. Mirrors become windows. Windows become memories. I am everywhere and nowhere, present and absent. Every heartbeat fractures into multiple rhythms. Every breath carries multiple intentions. Every glance contains entire conversations never spoken.

I attempt to name the loss. It evaporates. Naming is linear. Dreams are infinite.

I see a version of her, eyes soft, luminous. She reaches toward me. Not for me, not from me, but for the potential that never existed. The touch is imagined, impossible, and utterly real. It lingers on skin I no longer recognize as my own.

Her fingers trace my jawline in the dream. I remember this touch—the real version of it. After we'd made love, she'd trace my face like she was memorizing it, her fingers light, reverent. "I want to know every detail," she'd whispered.

Time fractures further. Days and nights fold into one another. Music I cannot identify drifts from somewhere beyond walls. Shadows of rooms I have never entered ripple into my vision. I feel the echo of my son, the sideline, the gyms, the cafés—all condensed into the single pulse of the dream.

And here, in this dream, I am free. Free from replacement, free from expectation, free from the gravity of reciprocity lost and impossibility unresolved.

The fractured room, the parallel room, the rooms of reflection—they have collapsed into something greater: **a liminal space where memory, imagination, and desire coexist without hierarchy**.

I lie still, feeling absence as presence. I feel potential as substance. I feel the infinite layered selves merge with my body, my chest, my pulse.

And I understand: sleep is not rest. Sleep is the room extended, fracturing further, dissolving into the subconscious, a **fantasy world that sustains all the realities I cannot hold awake**.

I float there, suspended. The light bends. Shadows multiply. Voices echo. Faces, absent and present, glance, smile, vanish.

And I do not wake.

Because the dream is home.

Because here, absence is luminous.

Because here, heartbreak is not a wound. It is architecture.

CHAPTER TWELVE

Summer Without Departure

The dream does not move forward.

It prepares.

I am always about to leave.

The air is warm—late afternoon summer warmth, thick with possibility. Light stretches long across streets I recognize but cannot place. There is luggage somewhere nearby. I know this without seeing it. Bags packed carefully, deliberately, as though intention itself has weight.

I am going somewhere.

I never go.

I stand in a house that feels temporary. Not unfamiliar, but not mine. Windows are open. Curtains breathe with slight breeze. Outside, cicadas hum in rhythmic insistence, marking time without caring whether I move through it.

Someone—perhaps her, perhaps no one—has suggested the trip.

"It will be good for you," the voice says. Not persuasion. Assumption.

I nod.

In the dream, I always agree.

I remember us planning a trip once. She'd pulled up flights on her laptop, comparing prices, talking about this beach town she'd always wanted to visit. "We should go in August," she'd said. "Before the semester starts. Just us."

The way she said "us" with such confidence. Like it was already established, already certain.

We never booked it.

I walk from room to room, checking things that do not need checking. Phone charger. Wallet. Keys. Passport. I pick them up, put them down, pick them up again. Each action carries the gravity of departure without the consequence.

Time behaves strangely here. It expands around preparation. Hours pass without progress. The sun shifts slightly, but never sets. Summer remains suspended, eternal, unresolved.

My daughter appears briefly. "Are we leaving soon, Dad?"

"Soon," I say. But soon never arrives.

She disappears. Was she ever really there?

I step outside.

The street is quiet. Too quiet for a day meant for travel. Cars are parked, unmoving. A bus appears at the end of the block, idling. I feel the familiar tightening in my chest—the moment before movement.

I do not approach it.

Instead, I notice details: the heat rising from pavement, the faint smell of sunscreen, a distant sound of laughter that never becomes visible. These sensations anchor me in the moment, hold me there.

I think of places I might go.

Coastlines. Cities. Airports filled with echoing announcements. Train platforms where departure feels ceremonial. Morocco, like we talked about. That music festival in California she wanted to attend. The quiet beach town with the good seafood restaurants.

Each image arrives fully formed and immediately dissolves.

The dream does not permit arrival.

I return inside.

The house has shifted. Furniture rearranged slightly. A room I did not notice before now exists. In it, sunlight pools on the floor, golden and inviting. The parallel room is here again, disguised as a summer interior.

She is present—but not as herself.

She appears as implication.

Her presence is embedded in the idea of the trip. In the way the suitcase was packed. In the assumption that this journey would have included her, or been inspired by her, or been a way of moving away from her.

I sit on the edge of the bed.

The suitcase is open now.

Everything is folded neatly. Too neatly. As if packed by someone who expects the contents never to be disturbed. I touch a shirt—the one I wore the night we went to the movies, the night I asked her to be my girlfriend. It feels real. Solid. Anchoring.

A thought surfaces, clear and calm:

If I leave, something will collapse.

Not catastrophically. Quietly. A room will cease to exist. A conversation will lose its echo. A future—unlived but intact—will finally dissolve.

So I stay.

In the dream, staying always feels like choice, even though it is inevitability.

Outside, the light begins to fade slightly, but not into evening. Just enough to signal that time is passing without progress. The cicadas continue. Summer insists. The heat holds everything in place.

I imagine sending a message to someone.

"I'm running late."
"I might not make it."
"I'll explain later."

No message is sent.

The dream resists explanation.

I walk again, aimlessly. A map appears briefly on a table. Routes highlighted. Destinations circled. I study it with interest, with hope. Morocco. California. The beach town. All places we talked about visiting together.

Then I fold it.

The bus outside pulls away without me. I watch it go through the window. There is no panic. Only a quiet recognition: this is how it always happens.

The dream is not about travel.

It is about **perpetual readiness**.

About living in the posture of departure without allowing the departure to finalize the loss. Summer remains because summer represents openness. Motion without consequence. Futures that remain technically possible.

I lie down again.

The suitcase remains open. The light remains warm. The idea of leaving remains intact.

And I understand, finally, why this dream repeats in sleep and in waking life:

Because as long as I do not leave,
the future I imagined has not been disproven.
As long as summer holds,
nothing is conclusively over.

The dream fades not into darkness, but into stillness.

Preparation without departure.
Movement without motion.
Love without reciprocity.

And somewhere, just beyond the edge of consciousness, the room waits—unchanged, patient, holding all the futures that never required me to arrive.

CHAPTER THIRTEEN

Micro-Awakening

I wake. Or think I do.

The room is familiar, yet slightly altered. Light enters differently—harsher, less forgiving, insisting on presence. The suitcase from the dream is gone. The sun is no longer suspended. Shadows fall predictably across the floor.

I sit up. Heart racing, pulse echoing. The air smells of morning, or maybe yesterday, indistinct but insistently real.

I check the clock. It reads a time I do not trust. Fifteen minutes late, thirty minutes late, an hour ahead. I am unsure if the day has truly begun, or if I remain halfway in the room of summer that refuses completion.

The panic rises slowly, methodically: I have forgotten something. Or someone. Or perhaps both.

My daughter. Did I forget to wake her?

Did I leave her at school? The thoughts come rapid-fire, irrational but insistent. I reach for my phone, check the time again, try to orient myself in linear reality.

My passport. Where is it? I need it for... what? There's no trip planned. But the dream lingers, insisting that departure is imminent, that I'm already late for something crucial.

I reach instinctively for my bag. My wallet. The weight of absence presses against my chest. My mind flickers between what is real and what lingers from the dream: did I actually leave her? Did I really board the plane? Or am I still suspended in the space between readiness and arrival?

Outside, the day moves forward without me. Cars pass. Birds sound alarmingly normal. The mundane march of the world continues while I negotiate these micro-awakenings. Each one is brief, impermanent, unresolved, leaving only the residue of tension and possibility.

I recall a flight—not from last night's dream, but from a real memory that feels dreamlike. My passport forgotten. The line of travelers moving ahead. Anxiety surging, escalating, a mirrored echo of the suspended summer dream. I am frantic, yet paralyzed. The world demands forward motion. I cannot obey. Not yet.

That actually happened. Two months ago. A conference I was supposed to attend. I'd packed, called a car to the airport, arrived two hours early. Only to realize at check-in that my passport was sitting on my desk at home. The flight left without me. I rescheduled, caught a later one, made the conference. But the panic of that moment—the absolute certainty that I'd failed at something basic, something everyone else manages effortlessly—stayed with me.

And then: realization.

This is not failure. Not really. It is rehearsal.

It is a continuation of the fractured room's logic: preparation without completion, engagement without resolution, the persistent awareness of absence shaping every heartbeat.

I sit again. Breathe. I feel her absence—my ex, my daughter in those irrational moments of panic, all the echoes—and I recognize that **micro-awakening is not interruption but reflection**. It is the overlap of waking life with the dream's architecture, where attention and desire persist across thresholds.

The suitcase appears in memory. The cicadas hum faintly from another dimension of time. The light refracts across walls that do not exist. I am simultaneously here, present in reality, and elsewhere, inhabiting absence, potentiality, and preparation.

I rise. Step toward the day. The sun is insistent. My daughter's presence—a blend of imagination and memory—guides my steps, reminds me of responsibility, of attachment, of love without completion.

The espresso coffee machine sloshes. I go through the motions—beans, grinder, water. Mechanical actions that anchor me in the present. She used to make me coffee. Not every morning, but often enough. She'd learned how I liked it—strong, no sugar, just a splash of milk. Small acts of care that accumulate into architecture.

And I understand: **micro-awakenings are the daily inheritance of the fractured room**. They are moments where absence collides with the world, where the dream's logic invades waking life, leaving behind small shards of impossibility, lingering futures, and unclaimed potential.

Each missed flight, each forgotten passport, each moment of being behind or late—these are **tiny proofs of the parallel room's persistence**. Proof that the mind cannot be constrained, that absence shapes presence, and that heartbreak, in its most profound sense, **never fully leaves**.

I step into the day. The suitcase is gone. The summer lingers. The light fractures. And I carry all of it, quietly, as though it were gravity itself.

CHAPTER FOURTEEN

When the Dream Is Verified

Morning comes early.

I run before the city decides what it is. Streets are empty, obedient, unremarkable. My body moves ahead of thought. This is deliberate. Running is how I quiet the mind—not silence it, but place it slightly behind me, like a shadow that cannot quite keep up.

Breath. Rhythm. Pavement.

The air is cool, almost cold. October settling in. My breath visible in small clouds. Each footfall a metronome, counting time without meaning.

Faces pass me occasionally—other runners, walkers, people carrying coffee cups with the seriousness of ritual. I register them without attaching meaning. Or I try to.

But the mind, even when positioned off, **continues its work.**

Here is what happened.
Here is what did not.
Here is what could have happened if she had stayed.

The scenarios arrive uninvited. Parallel tracks laid over the morning street. If she were here, we would have argued less by now—or argued more, worked through the inevitable friction of sustained proximity. If she were here, this run would be shared, or I'd be running alone anyway because she preferred yoga. If she were here, silence would mean something different—comfortable rather than punitive.

The thought ends the same way every time: she left without explanation.

That absence of narrative is heavier than departure. It refuses containment. It resists closure. It becomes a burden not because it hurts, but because it **demands constant interpretive labor**. The mind keeps trying to finish a sentence that no longer has an author.

I stop at a corner. Stretch my calves against a lamppost. Watch the light settle into the day.

A woman jogs past—ponytail, expensive running shoes, completely absorbed in her music. She doesn't see me. I watch her disappear around a corner, wonder briefly about her life, then let it go.

At the gym later, mirrors multiply the same problem. Bodies everywhere. Motion without intimacy. I lift, lower, repeat. Music pulses, anonymous and insistent. A woman passes me—different woman, different day, same echo. Another almost. I do not follow it. I have learned restraint. Or fatigue has learned it for me.

Then—without warning, without dream logic, without metaphor—she appears in the real world.

The commencement ceremony is formal, structured, designed to signify endings that feel earned. Caps. Gowns. Applause. Names pronounced clearly, deliberately. Closure staged as ritual.

She is there.

Not imagined. Not refracted. Not dream-assembled.

Real.

In the same room. Under the same lights. Seated within the same field of vision. Time behaves properly here. No fracture. No suspension. No distortion.

I am hooding students from my program. The procession is orderly, rehearsed. Each student approaches, I place the hood over their shoulders, we shake hands, they move on. Mechanical but meaningful. I'm focused on getting names right, on making eye contact, on being present for their moment.

Then I see her program listed. She's hooding students from a different department. My chest tightens. I scan the audience, trying to locate her before she takes the stage.

There. Three rows back. Talking to a colleague, laughing at something. She looks good. Professional. Put together. Like nothing ever happened. Like the compass and the vinyl and the three-hour phone calls were filed away in some drawer marked "brief mistakes" or "learning experiences."

My hands shake slightly as I hood the next student.

I grip the fabric tighter to steady myself.

Half an hour passes. My group is finished. I return to my seat in the faculty section, three rows from the front. I should leave. I could leave. Make some excuse about another commitment. But I stay.

Because I need to see her up there. I need to verify that she's real, that this all happened, that I didn't imagine the intensity of what we had.

When her turn comes, she walks to the stage with confidence. She's wearing academic regalia that fits her perfectly. She smiles at each of her students—the same smile she used to give me. Warm. Present. Generous with attention.

I watch her hood six students. Seven. Eight. Each interaction brief but genuine. She says something to one student that makes them laugh. Places the hood carefully on another. Adjusts it when it sits crooked.

I think about taking a picture. My phone is in my pocket. The impulse is strong—documentation, evidence, something to prove this moment existed.

My hand moves toward my phone.

What am I doing?

I stop myself. Literally pull my hand back. The urge is pathetic, invasive, wrong. I'm not entitled to images of her anymore. I'm not entitled to anything.

She finishes her group and returns to her seat. We're in the same room, breathing the same recycled air, participating in the same ceremony. The proximity is excruciating.

The keynote speech happens. Someone talks about resilience, about new beginnings, about the future stretching before us full of possibility. The words are well-meaning but land like clichés. I barely hear them.

After the ceremony, the crowd mingles. Families taking photos. Faculty congratulating students. I should leave. I need to leave.

But then we see each other.

Not accidentally. Not from a distance. Face to face in the hallway outside the auditorium.

Our eyes meet.

There is no surge. No collapse. No cinematic hesitation. Just recognition.

"Hi," she says.

"Hi," I reply.

It lasts seconds. Polite. Civil. Contained. Two people acknowledging shared history without reopening it. Nothing is explained. Nothing is repaired. Nothing is invited.

"Congratulations on your students," I manage.

"You too," she says.

Someone calls her name. A colleague. She turns, waves, looks back at me briefly.

"Take care," she says.

"You too."

And that's it. She walks away. I stand there for a moment, then walk in the opposite direction.

And yet—this is the most destabilizing moment of all.

Because reality confirms what the dream could not resolve: she exists independently of my fracture. She moves forward without the room, without the summer that never left, without the preparation that never completed.

The dream did not invent her.

The dream preserved me.

I sit through the rest of the afternoon in a fog. Drive home. Park. Sit in the car for twenty minutes before going inside.

The verification is complete: she was real. What we had was real. And she ended it anyway, with the casual efficiency of someone closing a browser tab.

That night, the dream tries to return. But it hesitates. Reality has intervened. Not to correct it—only to remind it that what was lost was not imaginary.

I understand something new now.

The burden is not that she left.
The burden is that she left **without narrating the ending**, and then re-entered reality as though the story were complete.

For her, perhaps it is.

For me, the dream continues—not as fantasy, but as **unfinished architecture**, carried into runs, gyms, ceremonies, mornings.

The difference between dream and reality is not clarity.

It is permission.

Reality permits no continuation.
The dream permits none to end.

And so I live between them—awake, moving, functional—while the parallel room hums quietly beneath consciousness, holding what was never denied, only never returned.

CHAPTER FIFTEEN

The Weight of Presence

The day unfolds with precision, ceremonial and bright. A week has passed since the commencement encounter. Seven days of carrying that brief "hi" and "take care" like stones in my pockets.

I'm at a DJ event. Not performing—not yet. I arrived early to check the setup, to watch the opening acts, to let the music settle my nervous system back into something resembling normal.

The venue is packed. Bodies moving to house music, the bass thudding through the floor into my chest. Lights pulse in sync with the beat. The energy is good—people here to dance, to lose themselves, to exist fully in the present moment.

That's what I love about these spaces. No one cares about your past. No one asks about your heartbreak. You show up, you play, you leave. Clean. Transactional. Present-focused.

Volta is headlining tonight. I knew this when I accepted the booking. She played the night before at a different venue—I heard she killed it. Now she's here, and I'm scheduled after her, which is both honor and pressure.

I see her setting up. She's focused, professional, checking levels, cueing tracks on her laptop. She looks exactly like she did the first time I saw her—stunning, confident, completely in her element.

My son had pointed out her name when I mentioned her. "Volta? That's cool, Dad. She was named after the battery guy Alessandro Volta and you have that song called volt!"

Yeah. Cool. A synchronicity I couldn't ignore even if I wanted to.

She finishes her soundcheck and walks toward the bar. I'm standing nearby, and our eyes meet.

"Hey," she says, genuine smile. "You're playing before me, right?"

"Yeah," I say. "I heard you last night. Everyone said you killed it."

"Thanks. I had fun." She orders a water. "What are you playing tonight?"

We talk. Ten minutes. Fifteen. The conversation flows easily. She's smart, articulate, passionate about the music. We discuss production techniques, Ableton, favorite labels, tracks we've been playing. She asks about my releases—she's heard the darkstep track, says she respects the sound design.

"We should collaborate sometime," she says. "I've been wanting to work with someone who understands that darker aesthetic."

"Absolutely," I say. "I'd love that."

And I mean it. The conversation is good. She's engaging, interested, interesting.

But underneath the ease, there's something else. A calibration happening in real-time. Am I being too eager? Too reserved? Am I reading this right? Is she just being professional, or is there something else?

She's younger than I am. A lot younger. Maybe in her thirties. I'm ten or fifteen years older. The age gap creates a gravitational field I'm acutely aware of. I don't want to be that guy—the older man misreading professional friendliness as romantic interest.

The music shifts. Her set is about to start. She excuses herself, heads to the stage. I watch her work—masterful mixing, reading the crowd perfectly, building energy with precision. She's in complete control up there.

I could stay. I watch her whole set. Could talk to her afterward, extend the conversation, see where it goes.

Instead, I find myself walking toward a group of my students who showed up to support me. "Hey guys," I say, forcing enthusiasm I don't quite feel. "Thanks for coming."

They're excited, asking about my set, buying me a drink I don't want. I engage with them, answer questions, play the role of the professor who DJs on weekends, the cool academic who straddles both worlds.

But inside, I'm wondering what the fuck I'm doing.

Volta is up there, brilliant and alive. We had a genuine connection in that conversation. She suggested collaboration—an opening, an invitation to continue talking. And I walked away.

Not because I wasn't interested. But because I felt **lost**. Like I'd misplaced the map for how to talk to women, how to navigate attraction, how to be present without the weight of everything I'm carrying crushing the moment.

Twenty, thirty minutes pass. I could go back. The students don't need me here. They're fine, dancing, enjoying themselves. I could return to the DJ stage, tell Volta her set is incredible, pick up where we left off.

I don't.

I stay with my students, safe in the familiar role, until it's time for my set.

When I get on the stage, I can feel it immediately—the confidence returns. Up here, I know exactly what I'm doing. The equipment is familiar, the crowd is mine to read, the music flows through me without hesitation. For ninety minutes, I am fully present, fully capable, fully myself.

Volta watches from the side of the stage for a few minutes, nodding approval at my track selection. She gives me a thumbs up, mouths "killing it," then disappears back into the crowd.

After my set, I pack up quickly. She's somewhere in the venue, probably talking to other artists, networking, being the professional she is. I could find her. Should find her, probably.

I leave instead.

Drive home in silence. Park in my driveway. Sit there, hands on the steering wheel, wondering what's happening to me.

The confidence I have on the stage doesn't transfer. The ability to be present, to make decisions, to trust my instincts—it's compartmentalized, trapped in this one context where the rules are clear and the outcomes are measurable.

Outside that context, I'm second-guessing everything.

Was Volta interested? Was I projecting? Would reaching out about collaboration seem desperate?

Would it be genuine professional interest or thinly veiled romantic pursuit?

The questions spiral. Unanswerable. Exhausting.

I think about the compass, still sitting in my desk drawer. About the way my ex used to text me constantly, making everything feel certain and clear. About how that certainty vanished overnight, leaving me unable to trust my own read on situations.

This is what heartbreak does. It doesn't just remove the person. It removes your confidence in your ability to interpret connection, to gauge interest, to move forward without constantly checking your footing.

I go inside. The house is quiet. My kids are with their mother this weekend. It's just me and the residue of another missed opportunity.

Not with Volta specifically. But with myself. With the version of me who used to be able to talk to women without this constant monitoring, this exhausting self-surveillance.

The parallel room waits. I don't enter it tonight. Don't need to. The message is already clear:

The burden is not just her absence.

The burden is what her absence revealed—the fragility of my own calibration, the way certainty can be withdrawn so completely that you forget what it felt like to possess it.

I am not over this.

Not even close.

And pretending otherwise—going through motions, accepting bookings, showing up at events—doesn't change the fundamental fact:

I am carrying a future that has nowhere to land, and until that weight finds distribution, every new possibility feels like threat.

CHAPTER SIXTEEN
Heartburn and Residue

Three and a half months have passed.

Time, that supposed healer, has not. It moves. I move. Yet the wound—less a wound than a furnace—remains hot.

The commencement encounter loops in my mind on repeat. Her casual "hi." The way she looked at me like I was any colleague, any acquaintance, any person she used to know but doesn't anymore.

The DJing encounter loops too. My retreat. My inability to stay present when possibility appeared.

Both confirm the same truth: I am not functioning at normal capacity.

I see her again—my ex, not another woman. Not in person this time. On social media. A friend's post tags her. She's at the commencement event, smiling, looking happy and unburdened.

The exterior world continues.

My interior world pauses, fracturing, replaying. The air carries the faint echo of past intimacy: the compass she gave me, the dinners, the care I offered when she was sick, the small gestures of attention I thought mattered. All catalogued in memory, all abruptly nullified.

I remember the vinyl store vividly. It's one of those memories that plays in high definition. We'd gone on a Sunday afternoon, both of us with nothing pressing, just wandering through the aisles. She'd pulled out album after album, reading liner notes, telling me stories about songs she loved.

She stopped at Nine Inch Nails—*The Downward Spiral.*

"I love this one," she said quietly. Held it for a moment, studying the cover art. Then put it back.

The way she said it—not performative, not hinting. Just sharing a fact about herself.

The next day, I went back alone and bought it.

When I gave it to her, she stared at it, then at me.

"You remembered."

"Of course I remembered."

She pulled me close and whispered against my neck: "No one has ever taken care of me like that."

That sentence. Those exact words. They're branded into my memory.

No one has ever taken care of me like that.

And then she discarded me like I was nothing. Like all that care, all that attention, all that presence meant nothing once she decided it was over.

I do not blame her, not entirely. People are allowed to change their minds. But the suddenness—after I had asked her to be mine, after laughter and conversation and mutual desire—shuts down every rational mechanism I have. Reciprocity, attention, shared joy: all erased overnight.

I move forward, yet the residue remains. Heartburn. Fatigue. Psychic overload. The ability to navigate new encounters with clarity is compromised.

Confidence, that carefully cultivated tool, becomes weaponized in reverse—it cannot show, cannot reveal vulnerability, cannot betray attachment.

The DJ event with Volta keeps replaying. Ten, fifteen minutes of good conversation. Real connection. Professional interest that might have been personal interest. And I walked away because I was **afraid**. Not of rejection—of misreading. Of making someone uncomfortable. Of being the desperate guy who mistakes professional courtesy for romantic possibility.

The mind splits between these temporal layers. Commencement, past intimacy, the DJ event, repeated micro-awakenings. All form a lattice of fatigue and desire. The fracture extends: not just heartbreak, but **the lingering moral weight of care given and not returned**.

It is not resignation. It is exhaustion. A body carrying the cognitive imprint of generosity, attachment, and trust denied.

I lie awake at night, memory after memory replaying:

Compass. *So you can pray at my place.*

Dinners. *You took care of me. No one ever does that.*

Vinyl. *You remembered.*

Three-hour phone calls. *I don't want to be careful with you.*

The movie theater. *Will you be my girlfriend?* Her smile. Her yes. The way she kissed me.

Then silence. Absolute, disciplined silence. Messages read and not answered. Access revoked without explanation.

Every trace magnifies the incoherence: why does the mind preserve reciprocity that was never reciprocated? Why does the body remember care that was retroactively nullified?

I breathe. I acknowledge. I feel the weight. Heartburn, fatigue, desire, absence.

The room within me, the fractured room, expands and contracts.

Memory and imagination overlap. Reality and dream continue their dialogue.

And I understand: the heartbreak is not measured by the days since it ended, nor by the clarity of explanation. It is measured by **the presence of everything that was invested and suddenly rendered invisible**, and by the **capacity of the psyche to continue carrying it**, even when reason demands it be left behind.

This is **the architecture of residue**. The weight of loving fully, honestly, openly—and being shut off without reason.

CHAPTER SEVENTEEN

The Sentence Without Appeal

The room is smaller now.

Not darker—smaller. As if the walls have moved inward while I was away. The light is unchanged, pale and undecided, coming from nowhere and everywhere at once. No windows. No doors. Just the table again. Two chairs. Distance calibrated precisely so that neither closeness nor escape is possible.

She is already there.

Not waiting. Not surprised. Simply present, as if presence were never in question.

I sit.

We do not greet each other. That ritual belongs to the living world, where politeness disguises rupture. Here, there is no need.

"You said," I begin, "that you wanted to part ways so you wouldn't hurt me."

She does not interrupt. That matters. In this space, she cannot go silent mid-sentence. Cannot withdraw without warning. The rules are different here.

I continue.

"That sentence has followed me. It pretends to be mercy. It performs kindness. But it is a sentence without appeal."

She looks at me then—not defensively, not apologetically. Just looking.

"You didn't want to hurt me," I say, "yet you removed explanation, continuity, recognition. You turned intimacy into something disposable overnight. That is not the absence of harm. That is **the concentration of it**."

The room does not react. It never does. It exists to hold statements once they are finally accurate.

The light shifts slightly. The shadows on the walls deepen. Time passes here, but without urgency.

"I didn't deserve this," I say. Not pleading. Declarative. "Not because I was perfect, but because I was present. I was attentive. I was generous with care. I showed up in ways people claim to want."

I pause. The fatigue presses against my sternum, familiar now, like gravity.

"You let me ask you to be my girlfriend," I say. "You accepted that future, even briefly. And then you withdrew everything—tone, warmth, curiosity—as if a switch had been flipped. No fight. No rupture. No warning."

She shifts slightly in her chair. The wood creaks. That is all.

"I am not here to ask why," I say. "Why belongs to people who still believe closure is something another person grants. I am here to name what happened."

The room feels tighter now. Focused. The air denser.

"What you did was not dramatic. That's the problem. It was quiet. Clean. Administratively efficient. You ended something alive without acknowledging that it had been alive at all."

She opens her mouth, then closes it. I do not invite her in. Not yet.

"You said you didn't want to hurt me," I continue, "but what you really meant was that you didn't want to witness the consequences of your decision. Hurt was outsourced. Deferred. Delivered without explanation."

I feel the burn again—not rage, not grief. **Recognition.**

"You took away reciprocity after confirming it existed. You removed the future without letting it decay naturally. You turned memory into debris."

The light flickers—not visibly, but internally, the way certainty does when it finally aligns with experience.

I think of the compass again. How it represented not just prayer, but permanence. A future where my presence in her space was assumed, welcomed, integrated. She gave me that future with a physical object, made it real and tangible. And then revoked it without ceremony.

"This isn't healing," I say. "This is accounting."

I lean back.

"I will carry the compass. The dinners. The vinyl record. The care. Not as proof of worth—that's beneath me—but as evidence that what existed was real, even if you decided to behave as if it wasn't."

She finally speaks. Her voice is calm. Almost kind.

"I didn't want to hurt you."

I nod. Slowly.

"That sentence," I say, "is where cruelty learned to disguise itself."

The words hang there. Unanswerable. Final.

Silence settles. Not awkward. Final.

When I stand, the room does not dissolve. It never does. It waits. It always waits.

As I leave, I understand something with absolute clarity:

This is not a story about moving on.
It is a story about **surviving the erasure of meaning without consenting to self-erasure in return**.

And that understanding—cold, exact, unromantic—is what finally brings everything into focus.

CHAPTER EIGHTEEN

Carrying It Outside

The room does not protest when I leave.

It never does. It relinquishes its hold quietly, as if it understands that what was said there has already fulfilled its purpose. The burden does not disappear—it follows—but it no longer insists on secrecy.

Outside, the world looks ordinary. That is its cruelty and its mercy.

I have been hiding this. Not consciously, not dishonestly, but methodically. I learned how to function while carrying it. I taught classes. I played sets. I answered messages. I stood in crowds and laughed at appropriate intervals. I learned the choreography of appearing intact.

No one noticed.

That is the part that exhausts me the most—not the heartbreak itself, but how **well it learned to camouflage itself inside competence**.

There are people around me now. Colleagues. Friends. Students. Strangers on sidewalks. None of them know that something unresolved has been traveling with me, pressing against my ribs, reheating itself at random moments. They do not know about the compass. Or the record. Or the sentence that disguised cruelty as care.

And I did not tell them.

Not because I am ashamed, but because heartbreak without spectacle does not translate well. It resists anecdote. It refuses summary. It sounds excessive when spoken plainly and trivial when softened.

So I carried it alone.

Until now.

I walk through the city with it exposed—not announced, not explained, simply no longer hidden.

It shows up in my posture, in my pauses, in the way my attention drifts when I pass couples who are still inside futures they trust.

I do not interrupt conversations to tell my story. I do not recruit witnesses. This is not disclosure as performance.

This is something quieter.

A refusal to pretend that nothing happened.

At the gym, a woman sits beside me. We exchange nods. Nothing more. The encounter ends exactly where it should. The burden does not demand projection.

At a crosswalk, a stranger glances at me, then away. The moment does not metastasize into fantasy.

I am learning something difficult and precise: **the burden loses power when it is allowed to exist in daylight without explanation.**

I no longer ask myself why she did what she did. That question belonged to the room.

Outside, it has no function. What matters here is different.

What matters is that I loved attentively. That I acted with care. That I offered continuity honestly. And that none of those things require retroactive permission to remain true.

The cruelty of the breakup does not need to be dramatized to be real. It does not need witnesses to be valid. It only needed to be named accurately—and then carried forward without secrecy.

I stop at a café. I sit alone. The chair across from me remains empty, and for once, it does not demand occupation. The absence is still there, but it no longer argues with me.

I order coffee. Watch people come and go. A couple sits two tables away, leaning into each other, sharing something on a phone. They laugh together. The ease of it. The assumption of continuity.

I don't feel envy, exactly. Just observation. They're in a different timeline. One where reciprocity holds.

Where the future they're building will be honored, or at least ended with dignity if it isn't.

I realize then that this is not closure.

Closure implies completion. Resolution. A sealed ending.

This is **integration**.

The burden is no longer quarantined in a private room where it grows distorted.

It moves with me now, proportioned, finite, survivable. It does not dominate the day. It simply occupies part of it.

And that is enough.

I do not forgive her. I do not condemn her. I do not rewrite the past to make it cleaner.

I live.

With the full knowledge of what was given, what was withdrawn, and what remains intact despite both.

The room still exists.

But it no longer owns the truth.

EPILOGUE

If

If there is another woman one day,
she will not arrive as repair.

She will not replace anyone. Replacement was never the problem. The problem was erasure.

If she appears, it will be slowly. Through conversation that does not rush toward meaning. Through shared silences that do not demand explanation. Through a future that forms without rehearsal.

I will not bring her into the parallel room. That room belongs to a specific fracture in time. It earned its walls. It keeps its silence.

But I will know—quietly, without comparison—that something has changed.

Not because the past has loosened its grip,
but because the future no longer needs to argue with it.

If I hold her hand, it will not feel like proof. It will feel like permission—to continue, not to correct.

She will not ask what broke me.
She will notice how carefully I carry things.

And if we plan something—travel, summer, a day that extends beyond itself—I will let it remain unfinished without panic. No passports forgotten. No last-minute awakenings. Just time moving forward, unafraid of itself.

If there is love again, it will not justify what was taken from me.

It will simply exist.

And that will be enough.

#TheParallelRoom

ABOUT THE AUTHOR

Haris Alibašić is a university professor and author. He teaches strategic management, ethics, and political economy. He researches AI governance, sustainability, resilience, and hybrid intelligence. His academic work has earned him elite global rankings in sustainability, resilience, and local government research. He has authored five books on governance, strategic management, hybrid intelligence, and sustainability. His academic career reflects sustained engagement with teaching, research, and public discourse, with an emphasis on critical thinking and intellectual integrity.

Haris' multidisciplinary creative whose work spans scholarship, music, and cultural production. Parallel to his scholarly work, Haris Alibašić is an active musician, producer, and DJ performing under the name **HAR!S**. His musical output includes multiple released albums and original productions that blend electronic, experimental, and genre-crossing influences, including darkstep, tech house, hardstyle, drum 'n' bass, and melodic techno.

HAR!S' work reflects a commitment to sonic exploration, narrative atmosphere, and emotional intensity, extending his storytelling beyond the written word into sound and performance.

Across both domains, Alibašić's work is marked by an insistence on originality, depth, and creative independence. Whether writing, producing, or performing, he approaches each medium as a space for inquiry, expression, and challenge to conventional boundaries.

A single father raising four children, he lives in Pensacola Beach, Florida, where he navigates the intersections of academic life, creative practice, and the architecture of loss. The Parallel Room is his first work of literary fiction.

www.ingramcontent.com/pod-product-compliance
Lightning Source LLC
LaVergne TN
LVHW090523110826
845146LV00003B/957

* 9 7 9 8 9 9 5 4 3 3 9 0 3 *